Nightmare in St. Martin's Lane

Jared Cade is the Amazon number one bestselling author of *Agatha Christie and the Eleven Missing Days*. He is a former tour guide for a bespoke luxury travel company, escorting parties around Agatha Christie's home, Greenway, which is now owned by the National Trust. During an appearance on the British television quiz *The $64,000 Question*, he won the top prize on his specialist subject of Agatha Christie's novels. Jared Cade is also the creator of the Lyle Revel and Hermione Bradbury mysteries. His work has been published in over a dozen languages.

Also by Jared Cade

Agatha Christie and the Eleven Missing Days

Murder on London Underground

Novella

Murder in Pelham Wood

Short Story

Where Silence Prays

Jared Cade

Nightmare in
St. Martin's Lane

SCARAB BOOKS

Published by Scarab Books
2023 © Jared Cade Limited
Jared Cade has asserted his right to be identified as the
author of this work under the Copyright, Designs and
Patents Act 1988.

ISBN 979-8-85479-450-3

Cover Design by GermanCreative

Nightmare in St. Martin's Lane

Lyle Revel sensed an ill-omen at the sound of scrunching tyres on the gravel outside Nettlebed. He was looking forward to spending a romantic night with Hermione Bradbury, but the arrival of the police changed everything. It was bewildering and infuriating to find himself being arrested by his old adversary DI Deveril.

'Lyle Revel, I am arresting you on suspicion of attempting to murder your ex-wife Taylor Fitzgerald. You do not have to say anything, but it may harm your defence if you do not mention when questioned something you may later rely on in court…'

Beneath Lyle's sweep of blond hair, his good

looks hardened with anger. 'Is this your idea of a joke, Deveril?' he demanded.

DI Deveril's dark eyes gleamed like a cobra's. 'I have strong reason to believe you've made three attempts on your ex-wife's life,' he rapped authoritatively.

Lyle was startled. *What the hell is going on?* he wondered. *Who in their right mind would harm Taylor?*

DI Deveril was accompanied by two of his own uniformed officers and a constable from the nearby village of Compton Sutton since Lyle's arrest was taking place in the county of Gosfordshire outside the Metropolitan Police's jurisdiction. Behind DI Deveril's back his work colleagues referred to him as 'the great oily bull' because he almost invariably got his man and was hell to work with until he had.

DI Deveril saw the redhaired girl standing next to Lyle Revel with the inscrutable expression on her Pre-Raphaelite face. It bothered him that Lyle Revel was one of those men who seemed to have all the luck when it came to attracting beautiful women.

The antagonism between the two men went back to that brief period in Lyle's life long before he had met Hermione when he had dated DI

Deveril's ex-girlfriend DS Penny Lane. The black-haired, bellicose inspector had borne a grudge against Lyle ever since.

Lyle gritted his teeth as a pair of cold metal handcuffs were snapped shut around his wrists. He looked at Hermione and his heart gave a sickening lurch. He would have given anything to spare them both this ordeal. *What must she be thinking?*

Hermione's attitude was one of dignified silence although inwardly she was just as shaken as Lyle.

'I'm going to do whatever is necessary to clear my name,' he told her.

Hermione replied in a surprisingly calm voice, 'It would probably be better if you said nothing until I call the family solicitor.'

Mr. Caldicott, the softly-spoken, white-haired solicitor summoned on Lyle's behalf, was waiting for him at Charing Cross Police Station in London.

'I hear you've landed in a spot of bother,' he said gravely. 'What's it all about?'

Lyle knew Mr. Caldicott reasonably well and was confident the solicitor would believe anything he told him.

'For the last five months I've been starring opposite Taylor Fitzgerald in a play called *Dead Reckoning*,' he replied. 'Sunday is usually the one day of the week I get off as an actor.'

'Only it's been ruined as a result of your arrest,' said Mr. Caldicott.

Lyle nodded bitterly. 'Several years ago the fashion designer Mario Berlusconi scored a publicity coup when Taylor agreed to model for him during London Fashion Week.'

As the actor was speaking an image of his ex-wife flitted across his mind. Taylor was a tall leggy blonde possessed of a Rapunzelesque beauty and a palpable sexual allure. Over the last two decades her glamourous looks, along with her style and elegance, had led to her gracing the covers of numerous magazines. In more recent years, she had consolidated her fame as a supermodel by becoming an actress and appearing on stage and screen.

'I remember reading about the case in the papers,' said Mr. Caldicott. 'At Mario Berlusconi's request, Cartier loaned Taylor Fitzgerald a fabulous necklace to wear during the fashion show's finale. It was stolen while she was absent from her dressing room trailer. The security guard keeping watch on it was found unconscious with a cracked skull.'

'He later died from his injuries in hospital,' said Lyle gravely. 'The police investigation was led by DI Deveril. Taylor was quickly eliminated from his inquiries. Mario Berlusconi had been involved in some questionable business transactions in the past. Deveril was convinced the fashion designer was guilty of stealing the necklace and killing the security guard. He was determined to nail Mario Berlusconi.'

'I gather you were one of the models in the fashion show and that's how you met Taylor Fitzgerald?' murmured Mr. Caldicott.

Lyle grinned. 'Taylor and I hit it off from the moment we met. The word torrid doesn't do justice to our roller coaster love affair. She soon confessed everything to me. Mario Berlusconi was her former lover. Three days after the robbery – before the security guard died – Mario Berlusconi told Taylor that he'd stolen the necklace so he could give it to her.'

'Did you tell the police what you knew?'

'I passed the substance of what I'd learned from Taylor onto my former girlfriend DS Penny Lane. After seven months of painstaking investigation, Mario Berlusconi was charged with robbery and murder. He went on trial at the Old Bailey. Deveril was confident of winning the case and being promoted to chief inspector. Under skilful cross-examination, DS Penny Lane admitted to having once had an affair with yours truly – Lyle Revel. Her revelation totally undermined her credibility as a witness and provided the defence team with the opening they needed. The case against Mario Berlusconi collapsed amidst a media frenzy. The Cartier necklace has never been recovered. It was probably cut up and sold on the black market.'

Mr. Caldicott gave an appreciative chuckle. 'You've never been shy when it comes to the limelight.'

'The case certainly ended my short-lived modelling career,' conceded Lyle ruefully. 'Luckily I was always the golden boy of amateur dramatics. Taylor and I went on to star opposite each other in a West End revival of *Tonight at 8.30*. The pressure of living in the media spotlight became too much and we divorced two years later. Deveril has always blamed me because Mario Berlusconi walked free. It's not in Deveril's nature to forgive and forget –'

At that moment DI Deveril burst into the interview room and sat down opposite Lyle. The usual tape recording procedures were implemented.

DI Deveril began, 'The most recent attack on Taylor Fitzgerald's life took place last night in St. Martin's Lane outside the Redgrave Theatre. *Why did you do it?*'

Lyle's nerves were on edge and it showed in his voice. 'I never went near her.'

'You followed a woman into St. Martin's Lane and knocked her unconscious. She was wearing a red dress just like the one Taylor Fitzgerald had changed into after the show. St. Martin's Lane is badly lit. What you didn't realize at the time is that *you attacked the wrong woman*.'

'I have no reason to harm Taylor,' protested Lyle. 'Or anyone else.'

DI Deveril refused to believe him. 'Your acrimonious divorce from her was splashed all over the newspapers several years ago.'

'If I had a drink for all the fake news the tabloids told about us I'd be a paralytic alcoholic six feet under,' insisted Lyle. 'Taylor and I have since moved on to different partners. She's now married to the formula one race car driver Jean-

Claude Toussaint.'

DI Deveril kept his needlelike gaze on Lyle's face. 'How satisfactory is your relationship with Hermione Bradbury?'

'If I had my way, I'd be with her right now,' replied Lyle. 'She's the most extraordinary woman I've ever known.'

'If your relationship with her is so terrific why are you currently starring opposite your ex-wife in *Dead Reckoning?* You've got the hots for Taylor Fitzgerald and you want her back.'

Lyle made a scoffing sound. 'Nonsense. Taylor and I are strapped for cash. We agreed to do a limited six month run of the play for want of any better career offers.'

'Your relationship with Hermione Bradbury must be superficial at best or you wouldn't want to expose her to the strains and jealousies of working opposite your ex-wife.'

'Hermione and I have absolute trust in each other.'

DI Deveril went on unperturbed, 'The back stage crew at the Redgrave Theatre overheard you trying to persuade Taylor to divorce her husband.'

Lyle kept a determined check on his emotions.

'That was over five months ago – during the final week of dress rehearsals,' he said impatiently.

DI Deveril smiled ferociously beneath the line of his black moustache. 'Witnesses heard you tell her, *"I know what's best for you. You'll regret it if you don't leave Jean-Claude. You need a man like me in your life."'*

Lyle leaned back in his chair. 'It's true – she does! I didn't say I was available myself.'

'Witnesses heard her reply, *"You're frightening me with talk like this. I want you to stop."* You were threatening her. Admit it.'

'Taylor is a bundle of nerves,' said Lyle. 'You can't place any reliance on what she says. Jean-Claude is a two-timing rat. He's got a girl hanging off each arm wherever he goes. Taylor deserves better. Ten to one she'll stay married to him and that will be the end of that. She was just letting off steam.'

Dislike radiated from every pore of DI Deveril's face. 'The very next day the first attempt on Taylor Fitzgerald's life took place. A piece of scenery came crashing down on the set during the final dress rehearsal. If she hadn't left the stage to speak to the prompt, the scenery would have landed on her. She might easily have been killed.'

'It was a nasty business,' agreed Lyle. 'I watched it happen from the wings.'

'The scenery fell on a part of the stage where you're not required to stand,' continued DI Deveril relentlessly. 'I suggest you booby-trapped the scenery so it would fall on your ex-wife. You've never forgiven her for the humiliation of divorcing you.'

'How was I supposed to have achieved that?' demanded Lyle. 'The stage technicians checked it out. They agreed it was an unfortunate accident due to a rope that hadn't been tied off properly.'

'Your ex-wife is a beautiful woman,' taunted DI Deveril. 'She's got you all steamed up. Her refusal to get a divorce from Jean-Claude Toussaint is driving you crazy. You just can't live with the fact that she belongs to another man and refuses to leave him for you.'

'This is all nonsense – pure speculation,' protested Lyle, shaking his head with frustration.

'Six weeks ago on the afternoon of Tuesday 18 January, someone almost ran Taylor Fitzgerald down outside her home in Holland Park,' said DI Deveril. 'You were the reckless driver in the silver convertible that sped off, weren't you?'

'No, I wasn't.'

'Where were you?'

Lyle spoke irritably. 'If you must know, I wasn't required at the theatre, so I spent the day doing various odd jobs around Nettlebed.'

'Can you supply any independent witnesses?'

'No, I'm afraid not. Hermione was shopping in London.'

'There must be a lot of silver convertibles on the road,' intervened Mr. Caldicott. 'This hardly amounts to irrefutable evidence against my client. London motorists are notoriously bad drivers. The car didn't hit my client's ex-wife, now did it? Perhaps she wasn't looking where she was going and stepped out into the road too soon. Her marital problems have been preying on her mind lately, after all.'

It was apparent from the way DI Deveril glared at Mr. Caldicott that he suspected the solicitor of white-washing the incident.

Turning back to Lyle, DI Deveril snapped, 'What time did you leave the Redgrave Theatre last night?'

Lyle frowned in an effort of recollection. 'I left a little later than usual. I stayed behind and chatted to the stage door keeper Arthur Moulton. We played a round of cards in his office.'

'Did you leave the theatre with anyone?'

'No.'

DI Deveril asked, 'Can you supply me with any witnesses who can prove you didn't follow a woman in a red dress into St. Martin's Lane and attack her in the mistaken belief she was your ex-wife?'

'No.' Lyle shook his head reluctantly. 'I never went anywhere near St. Martin's Lane. I turned left outside the stage door and walked up the street to the car park. I collected my car and drove home.'

'Have you any idea who might be trying to kill your ex-wife?'

'There's always Taylor's husband,' replied Lyle thoughtfully. 'Jean-Claude was angry when he learned she was going to star opposite me in *Dead Reckoning*. He seemed to think it was proof that we were having an affair. He's one of these arrogant men who think it's okay for him to cheat on his wife, but he objects to the idea of his wife cheating on him.'

DI Deveril's eyes narrowed. 'Are you telling me she's been unfaithful to him?'

'No, but it would serve him right if she had,'

said Lyle quickly. 'The media has gone into a frenzy suggesting Taylor and I must be sleeping with each other because we're appearing together on stage. It's pure speculation – nothing more. But Jean-Claude mightn't know that.'

DI Deveril questioned Lyle for another hour, then at his solicitor's insistence released him for lack of evidence.

'DI Deveril clearly doesn't trust you one little bit,' said Mr. Caldicott. 'I need hardly advise you to watch your step.'

'My inner voice is telling me the only way I'm going to get out of this mess,' said Lyle grimly, 'is if I solve the mystery of the original woman in red. My crime-solving skills are second to none so it shouldn't be too difficult. I'd give anything to know who this woman was and what she was doing in St. Martin's Lane….'

The following morning Hermione and Lyle were having breakfast at Nettlebed when they received a visit from DS Nicholas Snare of the Metropolitan Police. Beneath his short-cropped curly brown hair his solemn face broke into a wolfish smile.

'Lyle, I hear Deveril gave you a roasting last

night.'

'He was wasting his time, Nick,' said Lyle. 'I haven't the slightest idea who attacked the girl in St. Martin's Lane.'

He and Nicholas Snare had been friends for years. They both knew DI Deveril would have a fit if he discovered his best sergeant was consorting on his day off with the prime suspect in the case.

Over a pot of excellent coffee made by Hermione, Nicholas told them, 'The woman in red was – or rather is – Miranda Bell. Whoever followed her into St. Martin's Lane on Saturday night removed an empty champagne bottle from the rubbish skip outside the theatre and gave her a nasty wallop with it over the back of the head. She was found lying unconscious in the lane by a special constable who was on his way home. He did the usual heroic stuff. Called the police and the paramedics. The twos and blues arrived and cordoned off the area. Now here's the strange bit, Lyle. It's really up your street since you're into solving mysteries that no one else can unravel. As far as we know, *no one had a motive of any sort for attacking her.*'

Hermione asked hopefully, 'Were there any fingerprints on the champagne bottle?'

'There must have been because Deveril insisted on taking my fingerprints,' interjected Lyle.

'It's possible Miranda's attacker cut themselves on the jagged foil seal around the neck of the bottle,' replied Nicholas. 'Forensics found traces of blood on the seal. Once we find the owner of the fingerprints, a DNA comparison will almost certainly result in an arrest and a conviction.'

'Have you considered the possibility Miranda was attacked by a tramp?' said Hermione.

Nicholas shook his head. 'As far as theories go it's got too many holes. Miranda was wearing an expensive bracelet. Nothing was stolen from her or about her person. There was over four hundred pounds in her handbag which was found next to her body.'

'Perhaps Miranda was mistaken for a prostitute,' suggested Lyle.

'You can forget any ideas you have of some man knocking Miranda out cold and raping her,' said Nicholas, his voice heavy with relief. 'The hospital staff examined her. She's everything she claims to be. A twenty-one-year-old virgin from the Norfolk Broads without an enemy in the world. She's training to become a veterinary surgeon. It was her first visit to London. I should know. She's my niece.'

Lyle's eyebrows rose. 'Good God, Nick, I didn't realize you had a personal stake in this.'

'Is your niece badly hurt?' asked Hermione with a look of concern in her eyes.

Strong emotion rippled Nick's face. 'I saw Miranda in the ambulance before she was taken to hospital. She was still in her red dress. Her sloping shoulders were too weak to support her head. She suffered a nasty concussion. But no brain damage, thank goodness. Earlier in the night, she attended a performance of *Dead Reckoning*. She was accompanied by a friend from her school days. After the performance, the two girls went to the stage door. Miranda's friend Jilly Horton knows your co-star Declan O'Reilly. He was smitten with Miranda and invited both girls into his dressing room for a chat.'

Lyle gave a sudden surprised look of recollection. 'I remember overhearing Declan in the passage,' he said slowly. 'He was ushering a couple of giggly girls into his dressing room which is next to mine. It must have been Jilly and Miranda. I left my dressing room a couple of minutes later and went upstairs to play cards with Arthur in his office. Taylor popped her head in.

She was wearing a red dress. She said the cast were going out for supper. Would I like to come? I turned her down since I'd eaten earlier that evening. I think she went back to her dressing room to collect her scarf.'

Nicholas groaned and said, 'It's a shame the Redgrave Theatre is covered in scaffolding. The CCTV cameras in St. Martin's Lane have been disabled because the theatre is undergoing a 1.5-million-pound facelift. Miranda's attacker got clean away.'

Lyle spoke. 'When did Miranda and Jilly leave the theatre?'

'Declan O'Reilly invited them to join him and the rest of the cast for supper at the Ivy,' replied Nicholas. 'He swears they left the theatre ten minutes before he did. The Ivy Restaurant has a strict dress code so Jilly and Miranda decided to change into something more suitable. Jilly lives in a flat a short distance from the theatre. She gave Miranda a red dress to wear and helped her with her make-up and hair. She claims Miranda left the flat shortly before ten-forty-five. For some reason Jilly changed her mind and didn't go to the Ivy with her.'

'M'mm…' Lyle was thoughtful. 'I looked up

from playing cards with Arthur and glimpsed a woman in a red dress passing by the window. She entered St. Martin's Lane and that was the last I saw of her. I can't be sure of the time or whether it was Miranda or Taylor.'

'Which members of the cast dined at the Ivy?' asked Hermione.

'The entire cast with the exception of Lyle,' said Nicholas. 'Miranda had never met any of them before – apart from the object of her crush Declan O'Reilly. They had no reason to slip out of the Ivy and waylay her in the lane. She wasn't attacked for the usual reasons: robbery or sexual assault. Lyle, it appears to have been a motiveless crime – *unless one considers she was dressed like your ex-wife.*'

'Deveril mentioned Taylor had received an anonymous death threat,' said Lyle with an anxious look in his eyes. 'What can you tell me about it?'

Nicholas said, 'We interviewed Taylor at her home in Holland Park on Sunday afternoon within a few hours of her receiving the anonymous letter. She'd heard about the attack in St. Martin's Lane and was quite frightened.' He took a folded sheet of paper out of his pocket and passed it to Lyle. 'You're looking at a photocopy of the anonymous letter. The original is being held as evidence.'

Hermione looked over Lyle's shoulder and together they read the missive.

YOU'RE A SELF-CENTERED
WHORE WHO DESERVES TO DIE
TOO BAD I MISSED YOU IN
ST. MARTIN'S LANE

'The note was hand-delivered through the letter-flap in the front door of Taylor's home,' explained Nicholas. 'The person who delivered it got away without being seen.'

Lyle spoke. 'What account of the evening has Miranda given?'

'Her recollections are naturally rather fuzzy,' said Nicholas. 'She recalls entering the lane. Halfway along it she sensed someone was behind her, but before she could turn and look – wham! Someone hit her from behind. The next thing she remembers is regaining consciousness in the back of the ambulance. She says she has no idea why she was attacked and I believe her. Lyle, can you think of anyone who might want to attack Taylor?'

'My former wife is a beautiful woman who

enjoys stirring up strong emotions in others,' confided Lyle. 'Declan O'Reilly was furious when she dumped him after a brief fling a few years ago.'

'It's odd you're saying that,' said Nicholas slowly. 'After Declan O'Reilly arrived at the Ivy he remembered he'd left his wallet behind in his dressing room. It was less than a two-minute walk back to the theatre. He returned to the restaurant ten minutes later. It's possible he followed Miranda into the lane and attacked her...'

Lyle expelled his breath. 'Good God, I think we could be onto something at last…'

'Declan O'Reilly must have got quite a shock when Taylor turned up at the Ivy a short while later,' continued Nicholas. 'It would have been immediately obvious to him that he'd attacked the wrong woman. According to Taylor, he didn't seem his usual self during supper...'

It was Lyle Revel's intention to clear his name as soon as possible, but an attack of laryngitis, induced by a mild chill brought on by a burst of inclement weather, kept him away from the Redgrave Theatre until Wednesday. As soon as the matinee performance was over, he took Hermione backstage to his co-star Declan O'Reilly's dressing room.

Declan O'Reilly was a tall, wafer-thin Irish actor who specialized in playing suave, supercilious Englishman from amongst the upper middle-classes as well as the aristocracy. In real life he was much more down-to-earth and addicted to Botox to maintain his boyish charms which were three years on the wrong side of forty.

Lyle came directly to the point. 'I don't know how to tell you this, but the police think the wrong woman was attacked in St. Martin's Lane on Saturday night.'

Declan grew pale. 'Christ Almighty…are you saying Taylor was the intended victim?'

'Can you think of anyone who might want to harm her?' asked Hermione.

Declan gnawed his lower lip and then decided to come clean. 'It's no secret Taylor's marriage to Jean-Claude Toussaint is far from happy. I'm told he's got one hell of a jealous temper. They're always arguing with each other.'

'The police think the person who carried out the attack got an awful shock when Taylor later turned up at the Ivy,' added Lyle. 'Several people have stated you were startled by her arrival.'

Declan's temper flared. 'Surely you don't think *I* attacked the other girl – Miranda – by mistake? I'd just come from the restroom where I'd checked the messages on my mobile. Some investments of mine haven't done as well as they should. If fact, they've turned out bloody disastrously according to my accountant.'

'What can you tell us about Miranda Bell?' said Hermione.

'She was a sweet kid. In fact, I don't mind admitting I fancied the hell out of her. It was her first time in London. I thought I'd give her a thrill by inviting her to join the cast for supper at the Ivy. A mutual friend of mine brought her backstage after the show and introduced us.'

Lyle spoke. 'What's the name of your friend?'

'Jilly Horton. If anyone can tell you about Miranda, she can. She works for the fashion designer Mario Berlusconi...'

Mario Berlusconi's fashion house was just around the corner from the Redgrave Theatre. His assistant Jilly Horton, a gamine-faced woman with ginger hair and large glasses perched on the end of her petite nose, reacted with relief to Lyle's and

Hermione's news.

'I'm so glad Miranda is going to be all right,' she said, clutching a damp tissue to her face. 'What sort of brute would attack an innocent girl like that? How long did you say you'd known her?'

'Five years,' lied Hermione. 'Where did Miranda get the red dress she was wearing when she was attacked?'

Jilly's mouth trembled. 'Neither of us was properly dressed to pass muster in a restaurant as posh as the Ivy. We decided to come back to my flat and raid my wardrobe. Nothing upstairs fitted her properly which is why I hit on the idea of helping ourselves to one of the designer frocks out back in the storeroom.'

'Miranda must have been thrilled,' remarked Hermione. 'Am I right in thinking she was hoping to impress Declan O'Reilly?'

Jilly nodded and gave a watery smile. 'She was absolutely smitten with him when I took her backstage to meet him after the show. I dressed her in one of Mario's designs. A lovely red dress with shoulder pads. She looked stunning in the red shoes and handbag that went with it. I couldn't resist the temptation to lend her an expensive bracelet of mine.'

'Why didn't you go to the restaurant with her?' asked Hermione.

'We were about to leave the shop when I got an important business phone call. I urged Miranda to go on ahead without me.'

Lyle spoke. 'What time was that?'

'Oh, gosh…it must have been shortly before a quarter to eleven. I thought Miranda would be safe because the Ivy is such a short distance away. I was planning to join her there after I'd dealt with the business call. But no sooner had I hung up than Mario and Francois turned up. They'd dined with a client at the Ritz and looked very elegant in their tuxedos.'

'Preparing for the shows must keep you very busy,' said Hermione sympathetically.

Jilly released a frazzled sigh. 'I've been run off my feet. Francois recently broke his right arm and I've had to type and sign all his letters for him, too. I can't help feeling Mario and Francois are taking too many dresses to the Edinburgh fashion show. The models won't get to wear them all. Mario and Francois were quite angry when they heard I'd let Miranda leave here in one of their dresses. I didn't think it would matter if anyone saw her in it. I told them Miranda had promised to give it back but I'm not sure they believed me –'

'Well, well, well…who have we here?' asked Mario Berlusconi in a soft, dangerous voice as he emerged from the back regions of the shop.

Jilly flushed at the sudden appearance of her employer. Mario Berlusconi was as exotic as a dragonfly, with a pencil-thin black moustache and goatee beard. His talent as a fashion designer, along with his avant-garde style of dress, meant he was the darling of the fashion scene and paparazzi. His memory seemed to come to him.

'Why, of course, it's Lyle Revel.' Mario Berlusconi shook hands with him in an unexpected show of friendliness. 'I haven't seen you in years.'

The last time Lyle had seen the fashion designer was when he had testified against him at his trial. Mario Berlusconi appeared to bear no malice towards Lyle which under the circumstances seemed nothing short of extraordinary.

A thickset man resembling a bullfrog entered the shop from the street. His right arm was encased in a plaster cast and the leather bikers gear he was wearing made his complexion look twice as coarse. His piercing blue eyes, surrounded by surprisingly long lashes, narrowed in displeasure at the sight of his two work colleagues engaged in idle chat.

'Allow me to introduce my business associate Francois Fiocca –' began Berlusconi.

Nodding indifferently at their visitors, Fiocca turned to his business partner and spoke in an irritable, guttural voice. 'We haven't got much time if we're to get this latest collection ready for the Edinburgh show. We've already had one setback this week.'

Jilly winced apologetically. 'I'm really sorry about the red dress –'

'You will have to excuse my friend's lack of manners,' added Berlusconi smoothly. 'A couple of weeks ago he fractured his arm by coming off his motorcycle in a road accident –'

'It was entirely the other party's fault,' insisted Fiocca with a scowl.

'Lyle and Hermione called by to let me know Miranda is on the mend,' said Jilly with a strained smile. 'Isn't that wonderful news?'

'I've been mugged twice in the time I've lived in London,' said Fiocca disgruntledly. 'It was a waste of time going to the police. The culprits were never caught. Someone probably distracted the poor kid by asking her for a cigarette while their accomplice crept up on her from behind. The same thing happened to one of our models in New York. A pair of youths snatched her handbag and ran off. Muggings are rife in the Big Apple. She never got it back.'

'The police suspect Miranda was attacked in mistake for your former lover Taylor Fitzgerald,' said Lyle, gazing directly at Berlusconi.

The fashion designer started visibly. 'I can't believe anyone would want to harm Taylor,' he said coldly.

'She's a beautiful woman who's jilted a number of men,' said Lyle.

'One of them might have wanted to even the score,' suggested Hermione.

Berlusconi drew himself up haughtily to his full height. 'Get the hell out of here! I've had enough of your insulting suggestions. I've got a business to run.'

As their unwanted visitors left the shop, Fiocca turned angrily on his business partner. 'Have you been seeing Taylor again? I warned you *she's no good for you.*'

Outside in the street, Hermione paused to admire the pristine Harley-Davidson standing by the kerb. 'You certainly know how to draw strong reactions from people,' she remarked.

'There's never a dull moment when you're with me,' replied Lyle good-humouredly.

'Is that why Taylor jilted Mario Berlusconi in favour of you?'

'It's a long story and it doesn't get better with each retelling,' confided Lyle. 'Mario Berlusconi told Taylor he stole the Cartier necklace because he wanted her to have it. She became terrified of him after the security guard died from his injuries. Later in court Mario Berlusconi's defence team claimed he fabricated the story in an ill-advised bid to persuade her to marry him.'

'Did you notice how dilated Mario Berlusconi's pupils are?' asked Hermione. 'I shouldn't wonder if he's a drug addict.'

'The same idea has already crossed my mind,' said Lyle. 'Drug taking is rife in the fashion industry particularly among models.' He answered his ringing mobile. 'That was Nicholas Snare,' he explained after ending the call a couple of minutes later. 'He says we can cross Mario Berlusconi and Francois Fiocca off our list of suspects. They both have alibis for the first two attacks on Taylor's life.'

'How come?'

'On both occasions the pair were in New York on business. Their most recent trip to the big Apple lasted for three weeks. They only returned to London five days ago. Unfortunately, there was another attack on Taylor's life this morning. That explains why she missed today's matinee performance. I ought to have known something was wrong.'

Hermione asked with a sharp intake of breath, '*What happened?*'

'A masked intruder broke into Taylor's home at Holland Park. She was badly injured. The intruder got away before the police could be summoned...'

Lyle and Hermione found Taylor Fitzgerald resting in a private room at St Mary's Hospital in Paddington. The blonde's ribs were badly bruised and she was wearing a brace around her leg because she had ruptured her left Achilles tendon. Doctors had advised her that it could take four to six months to heal properly. Taylor's understudy would be playing her part in *Dead Reckoning* for the foreseeable future.

Jean-Claude Toussaint, a tall lithe man with a suntanned visage that resembled a box-faced

Pekingese, was bending solicitously over his wife. His eyes flashed with jealousy as Lyle entered the room with Hermione.

'Taylor, we heard what happened,' said Lyle anxiously. 'Have you any idea who did this to you?'

'I woke around seven o'clock,' replied Taylor in a subdued southern accent that hailed from Louisiana in the United States. 'As I came out onto the landing, an intruder grabbed me from behind with both his hands. I caught a glimpse of his balaclava just before he flung me down the stairs.'

'Did you notice anything unusual about the attacker that might help the police to identify him?' asked Lyle quickly.

Taylor shook her head and her eyes brimmed with tears. 'All I know for certain is that it was a man.' She turned to her husband Jean-Claude who was standing by her bedside holding her hand. 'I was lucky not to break my neck in the fall.'

She began sobbing.

'Taylor, there's no need to panic,' said Jean-Claude. 'We're going to get to the bottom of this, I promise you.' His face tightened with anger as he turned and looked at Lyle. 'What are you doing here, Revel?'

Lyle murmured, 'Jean-Claude, I had no idea you were back in London.'

'I flew in this morning. Taylor doesn't need you. She's got me.'

'She must be deeply reassured to hear you say that,' said Lyle calmly. 'In the past you've made it clear you care more for fast cars and fast women than your own wife.'

Jean-Claude grabbed Lyle by the lapels of his jacket. 'Your big mouth is going to land you in trouble one of these days, Revel!'

'Stop it!' protested Taylor. 'I've got the most awful headache.'

Lyle refused to be intimidated. 'It must have taken a strong man to pitch Taylor down the stairs,' he added.

'*It wasn't me.*' Jean-Claude glared at Lyle and reluctantly released his grip. 'My plane got into Heathrow at nine-thirty this morning – *satisfied?* Now get the hell out of here before I have you thrown out by security.'

As Lyle and Hermione left the room, they heard Jean-Claude speaking in a broken voice to his wife, 'It's going to be all right, darling. I – I promise not to go away like that again. Régine means nothing to me. It's over between her and me. From now on you're all that matters to me…'

Two hours later, Lyle received a call on his mobile from his best friend.

'You're no longer Deveril's favourite suspect,' announced DS Snare cheerfully. 'He's taken Jean-Claude Toussaint in for questioning.'

'Nick, this is the best news I've had all day.'

'Jean-Claude's declaration of love for his wife would be touching if it were genuine,' continued DS Snare. 'He lied about flying into Heathrow at nine-thirty this morning. He arrived late on Friday afternoon and booked into the Dorchester Hotel with his latest girlfriend – the super model Séraphine. She left him on Saturday afternoon. Jean-Claude claims he attended a poker game later that night but he's refusing to tell us where it took place or name the participants. His reticence could be due to the fact the game was illegal or the players are members of the criminal fraternity. There again, he might have carried out the attack in St. Martin's Lane. If he's not careful, he could find himself spending the night in a police cell. It doesn't pay to rub Deveril up the wrong way.'

'Jean-Claude is a jealous man,' said Lyle. 'He's also strong enough to have flung his wife down the stairs in a bid to kill her. Who found Taylor and rang for an ambulance?'

'The live-in housekeeper. She heard Taylor's scream, but didn't see the assailant. He got out of the house quickly.'

Lyle thanked Nicholas Snare for calling and rang off. He discussed the latest developments with Hermione.

'I can't believe Taylor's attacker is Declan O'Reilly,' she said. 'He hasn't worked in over a year. He would hardly risk the play closing by harming her.'

'M'mm…I don't think this case is as complicated as I first thought,' murmured Lyle.

'Taylor's attacker has got to be Jean-Claude,' insisted Hermione. 'Anyone can see he's a jealous nutcase. He can't handle the fact his wife is working alongside you – or Declan for that matter. Where are you going?'

'I ought to have realized sooner who sent the anonymous letter to Taylor,' said Lyle. 'I doubt if I'll have any difficulty getting a full confession from the culprit...'

He drove to St Mary's Hospital in his silver convertible, Lady Godiva, and entered Taylor's room.

'Jean-Claude won't be happy if he finds you here,' she began.

'That's why we're not going to tell him,' said Lyle calmly. 'He's currently being questioned by the police in regard to the attack in St. Martin's Lane. I don't believe for one moment there was an intruder in your house this morning.'

Taylor gazed at him with large, frightened eyes. 'What are you saying?'

'We both know Jean-Claude is the sort of man who only wants something when he thinks he can't have it,' said Lyle. 'You knew if he heard your life was in danger he would ditch his latest girlfriend and come back to you.'

A glimmer of admiration came into Taylor's eyes. 'I'm not masochistic enough to throw myself down the stairs,' she said with a shudder.

'Am I right in thinking you've been taking diet pills?'

'How did you know that?'

'You've been looking unusually pale lately,' replied Lyle. 'I think you had a dizzy spell, lost your balance and fell down the stairs.'

Taylor's eyes filled with tears as the memory reclaimed her. 'The story I told about a masked intruder was a pack of lies. I was clever to think that up before the paramedics arrived. How did you know I wrote the anonymous letter?'

'The letter stated *YOU'RE A SELF-CENTERED WHORE WHO DESERVES TO DIE*. Being an American you spelt self-centred with four e's. Here in England we spell it with three. It also struck me as odd that for someone whose life had supposedly been threatened four times you had only received the one threatening letter – and that was after the attack in St. Martin's Lane.'

'You must think I really am self-centred,' said Taylor wistfully. 'I still don't understand how you could have known it was me.'

'If the anonymous letter had been genuine,' said Lyle, 'you would have told me about it owing to my well-earned reputation for solving mysteries. The alleged attacks on your life defied credibility because they took place at such random intervals. The incident involving the falling scenery occurred over five months ago. You narrowly avoided being run over by an irate motorist six weeks ago because you were distracted crossing the road.'

'Where do we go from here?' asked Taylor in a tremulous voice that, in the blink of her sultry eyelashes, was capable of ditching her southern twang in favour of the upper crust English accent she had adopted for the vixen she had played in *Dead Reckoning*.

'The press don't know about the incident in St. Martin's Lane or the other alleged attacks on your life,' said Lyle. 'The situation would be a lot worse for you if they did.'

'I've still caused a lot of pain to the people around me.' Taylor released a self-pitying sigh. 'I'm not sure if I can live with myself.'

Lyle was unable to stifle an affectionate laugh. 'You usually do,' he said, ignoring a warning tingle in his loins.

Taylor's interest was piqued. 'What do you mean by that?'

'Jean-Claude is currently the number one suspect in the case,' said Lyle with a ring of satisfaction in his voice. 'The police are grilling him to within an inch of his life. We wouldn't want to spoil their fun, now would we?'

'I guess not…'

Lyle and Taylor exchanged conspiratorial smiles.

'Now I've dealt with your phantom assassin that brings me back to the original problem underpinning this case,' he added thoughtfully. 'What reason could anyone have for attacking an unknown twenty-one-year-old girl in St. Martin's Lane?'

'I haven't the slightest idea,' said Taylor bewilderedly.

Lyle believed her. 'It appears to have been a motiveless crime,' he said frowning, 'totally devoid of rhyme or reason – unless….' He fell silent for several moments then suddenly exclaimed in tones of quiet exaltation, '*Of course!* Why didn't I think of it sooner…?'

'Think of what?'

Lyle smiled enigmatically and strode out of the room without satisfying Taylor's curiosity. He pulled his mobile out of his pocket and press-dialled DS Nicholas Snare's number.

That night Lyle Revel gave a brilliant performance in *Dead Reckoning*. He wasn't disappointed that his ex-wife was no longer in the play. Taylor was an

egotistical, upstaging diva – but what a woman...
Mere words alone could not do justice to her
extraordinary beauty, charisma, talent or wit. He
would never regret having been married to her.
Jean-Claude Toussaint was a lucky man although
he was too stupid to know it.

As Lyle left the stage door of the Redgrave
Theatre, basking in the memory of the audience's
applause, he was accosted by a small throng of
autograph hunters. After satisfying their demands,
he walked a short distance to where Lady Godiva
was parked. He found DS Nicholas Snare waiting
for him. The latter's face was suffused with a look
of victory. After conferring with his friend, Lyle
drove home to Nettlebed and acquainted Hermione with the day's events.

'The individuals who attacked Miranda wanted
to remove the shoulder pads from inside her
dress,' he explained. 'They were filled with cocaine.
That's how Mario Berlusconi and his business
partner Francois Fiocca were smuggling the stuff
to Edinburgh to sell on the streets. As their
assistant Jilly told us, they were planning to take
too many dresses to the fashion show. You were
right to suspect there was a drug angle when you
saw Mario Berlusconi's dilated pupils. Earlier
today, Nicholas confided my suspicions to Deveril.

Police officers raided the shop tonight and found cocaine concealed in the shoulder pads of all the dresses.'

'How did you know Miranda was attacked for her shoulder pads?' asked Hermione, fascinated by what he was telling her.

'Nicholas saw Miranda in the ambulance after the attack,' said Lyle. 'She was still wearing the red dress. He told us, *"Her sloping shoulders were too weak to support her head."* His description didn't tally with Jilly's because she had stated *the dress had shoulder pads*. Since her employers' arrest, Jilly has been singing like a canary. Mario Berlusconi and Francois Fiocca turned up unexpectedly at the shop on Saturday night after dining at the Ritz and saw the red dress was missing. Jilly told them Miranda was wearing it and had just left the shop. Mario Berlusconi ordered Jilly to get on with some paperwork for their tax return. He and Francois Fiocca left the shop, still dressed in their tuxedos, claiming they had a business appointment. The pair went after Miranda and waylaid her in St. Martin's Lane.

'Am I right in thinking Miranda was struck by Mario Berlusconi?'

'On the contrary, we only ever had Mario

Berlusconi's word that Francois Fiocca fractured his right arm a couple of weeks ago in a motorcycle crash. The pristine Harley-Davidson belonging to him outside their shop obviously had not been involved in an accident. What's more, the pair had only just returned from a *three-week business trip to New York*. After knocking Miranda unconscious and retrieving the shoulder pads, Francois Fiocca somehow tripped and fell, fracturing his arm, as he fled from the scene of the crime. Later that night, he was admitted to St. Mary's Hospital in a great deal of pain. Staff put his fractured arm in a plaster cast and gave him some painkillers.'

'It serves the brute right,' said Hermione.

'On a happier note,' continued Lyle, 'Francois Fiocca left a clear set of his fingerprints behind on the champagne bottle. Since his arrest he's been obliged to remove his biker's gloves. The cut on his right hand was almost certainly caused by the ripped foil around the neck of the champagne bottle. DNA tests are expected to establish his guilt beyond all doubt.'

'What made you suspicious of the pair in the first place?'

'There was no media coverage of the assault in

St. Martin's Lane,' said Lyle, 'but earlier today Francois Fiocca told us, "*Someone probably distracted the poor kid by asking her for a cigarette while their accomplice crept up on her from behind.*" The only way he could have known Miranda was struck from behind is if he was involved in the attack.'

'You've been wonderfully clever,' said Hermione.

'There's one other piece of good news,' added Lyle. 'Miranda will be leaving hospital tomorrow.'

'Nicholas must be over the moon,' exclaimed Hermione happily.

Lyle grinned. 'Did I tell you Deveril has taken all the credit for solving the case?'

'It would serve Deveril right if you sued the Metropolitan Police for wrongful arrest,' said Hermione.

Lyle's eyes twinkled at her. 'I'll be sorely tempted to do just that if Deveril ever interrupts our Sunday night again,' he said, putting his arms around her. 'All I want to do now is make up for lost time by making love to you…'

THE END

Also by Jared Cade

Murder on
London Underground

Peter Hamilton, London Underground's managing director, is horrified when his ex-wife is pushed under a train.

Following the murder of a second commuter, he receives a phone call from an organisation calling itself Vortex that is dedicated to preventing the privatization of the network. "You were the intended victim at Baker Street… Next time you won't be so lucky…'

In desperation, Hamilton turns for help to Lyle Revel and Hermione Bradbury, a glamorous couple with a talent for solving murders.

But as the death toll rises, the terrorists release a runaway train on the network…

'A chilling thriller and a great read' – Louise Burfitt-Dons, author of the PI Karen Andersen series

Also by Jared Cade

Murder in
Pelham Wood

Pelham Wood is the perfect place for a romantic stroll for the crime-solving duo of actor Lyle Revel and cellist Hermione Bradbury…

Their discovery of a dead body on Hallowe'en results in a man being arrested for murder. The evidence against him is incontrovertible, but Lyle and Hermione have their doubts about his guilt.

As they set out to discover who the real killer is, they find themselves trapped inside a secret sex chamber with nowhere to hide.

Will they be able to rely on their wits to escape? Or are they destined to become one of the secrets buried deep in Pelham Wood…?

'An intriguing impossible crime with a first-rate solution… John Dickson Carr would have applauded' – Dempsey's Reviews

Printed in Great Britain
by Amazon

26960610R00026